JOHN CENA

ELBOW GREASE

ELBOW GREASE

FLASH

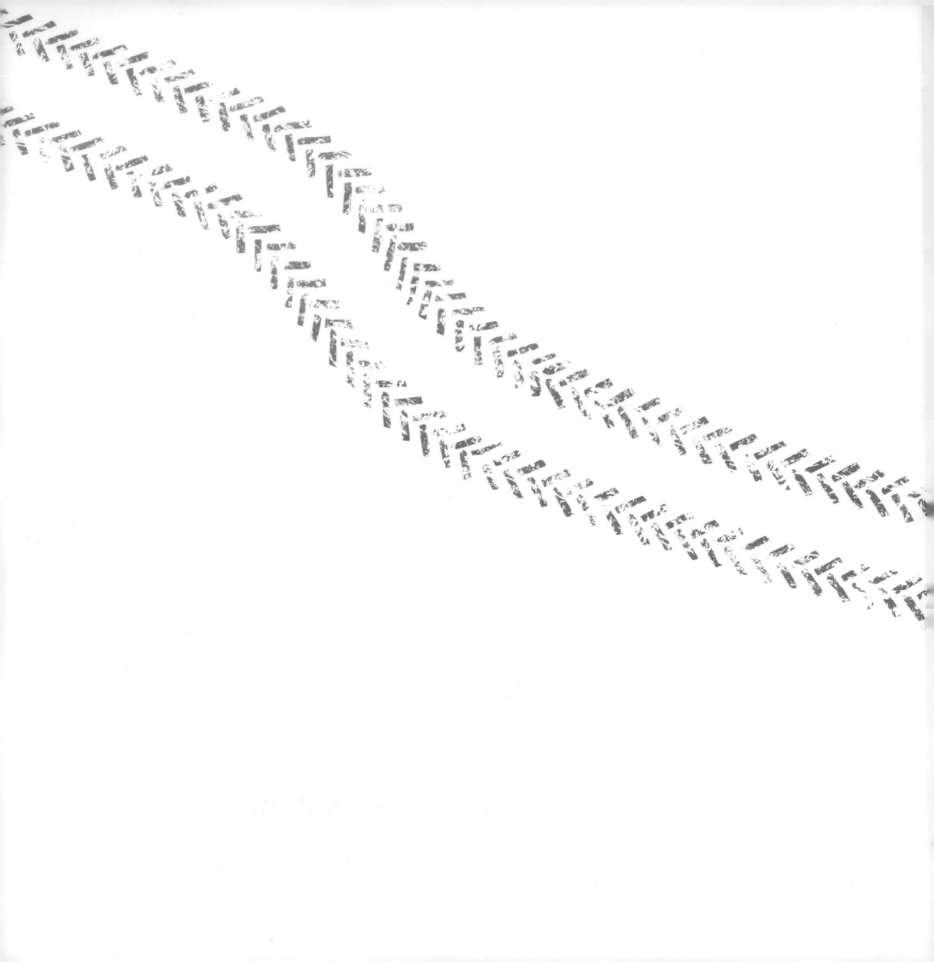

JoHN CENA
ELBOW GREASE

Hey, that's me!

Illustrated by Howard McWilliam

SCHOLASTIC INC.

Elbow Grease was the smallest truck in the Demolition Derby, but he never let that bother him.

Why should I?

His brother Tank was tougher.

His brother Flash was faster.

His brother Pinball was smarter.

His brother Crash was braver.

Okay, we get the point.

What Elbow Grease had was GUMPTION.

You got that right, Buster.

He always tried his best and never, ever gave up.

Ouch!

At night, Mel the mechanic plugged in Elbow Grease to charge while the other trucks slept outside. Sometimes his brothers teased him for being different.

Elbow Grease didn't get upset. He was glad to be inside, especially during storms.

The brothers laughed.

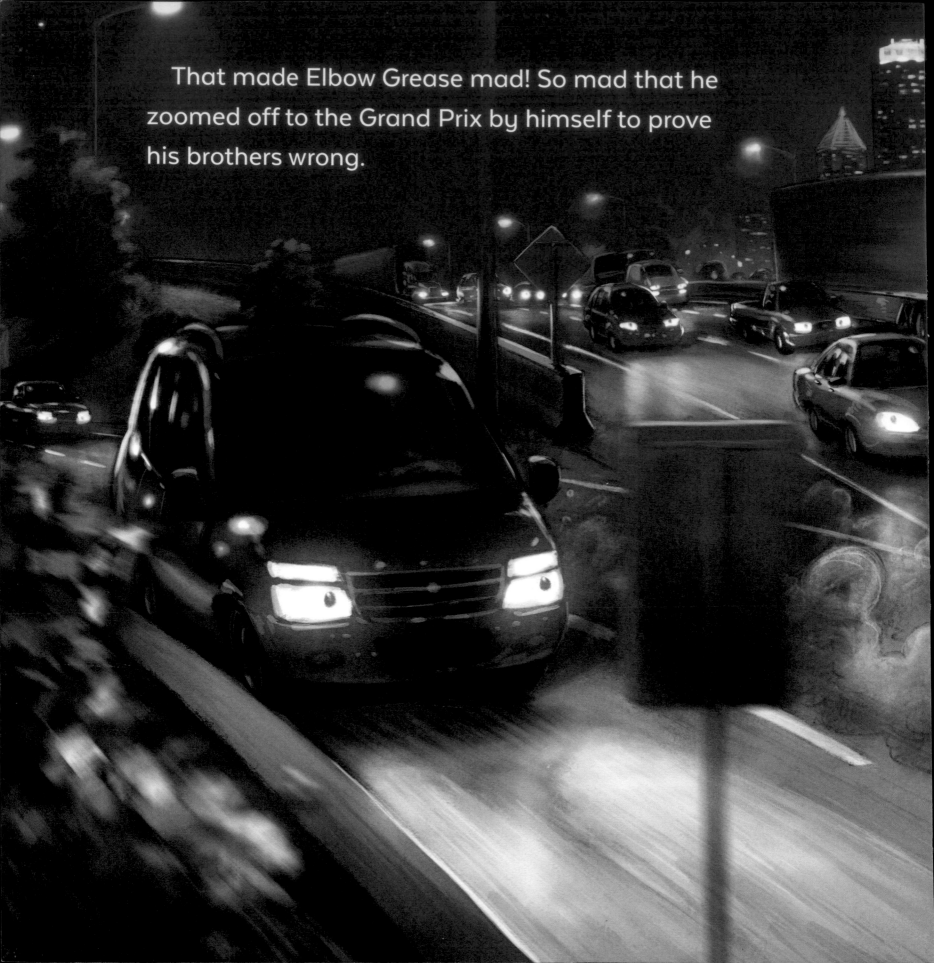

That made Elbow Grease mad! So mad that he zoomed off to the Grand Prix by himself to prove his brothers wrong.

In the morning, Elbow Grease was exhausted.
He had been driving all night without a charge.

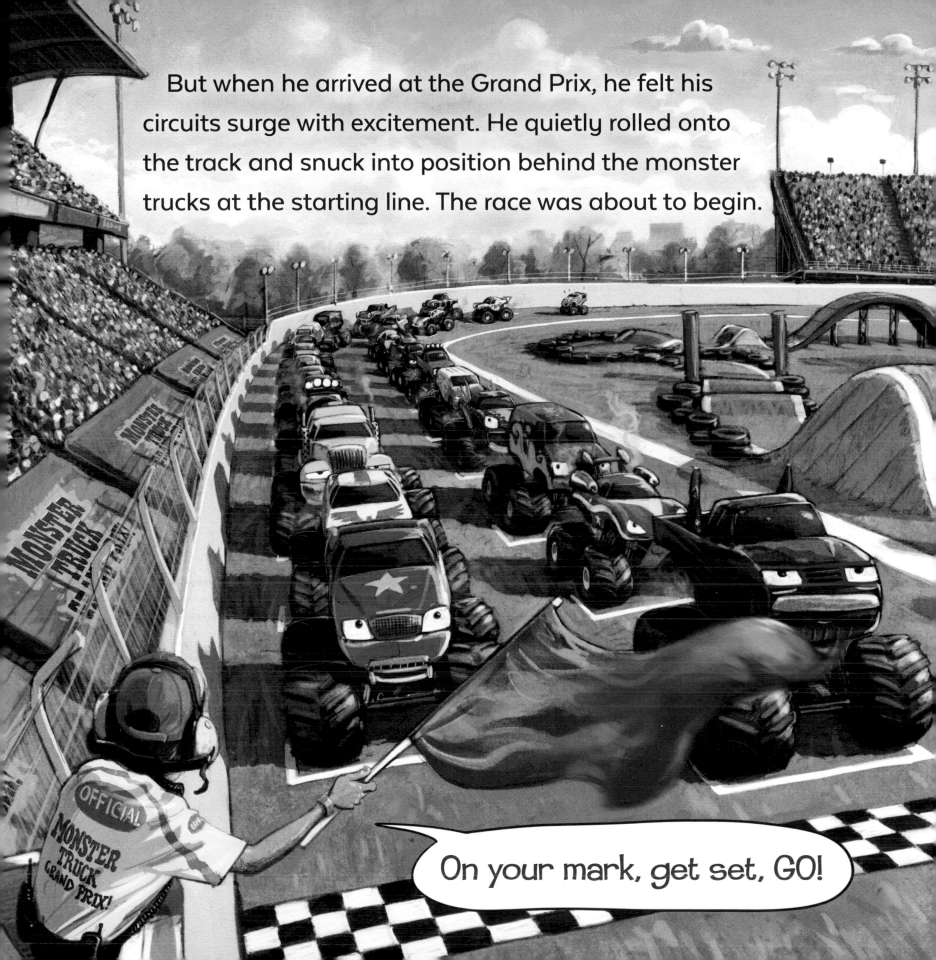

But when he arrived at the Grand Prix, he felt his circuits surge with excitement. He quietly rolled onto the track and snuck into position behind the monster trucks at the starting line. The race was about to begin.

On your mark, get set, GO!

The other trucks were bigger. The other trucks were faster. The other trucks had more experience and better technique.

He fell behind, but he kept on trucking.

He got covered in mud, but he kept on rolling.

He got bashed and smashed and even caught on fire
a little bit, but still—HE KEPT ON GOING!

Halfway through the race, it started pouring rain.
Thunder rumbled. Lightning flashed. All of a sudden,
Elbow Grease's engine shut down. His battery was
completely dead.

The lightning jolted the battery back to life! Elbow Grease barely had enough charge to keep going, but he didn't give up. He didn't give in. No matter what, he would finish this race—even if he came in last.

Mel and Elbow Grease's brothers arrived just in time to see him rattle across the finish line and collapse in a heap. The winner's celebration was already over.

THE END

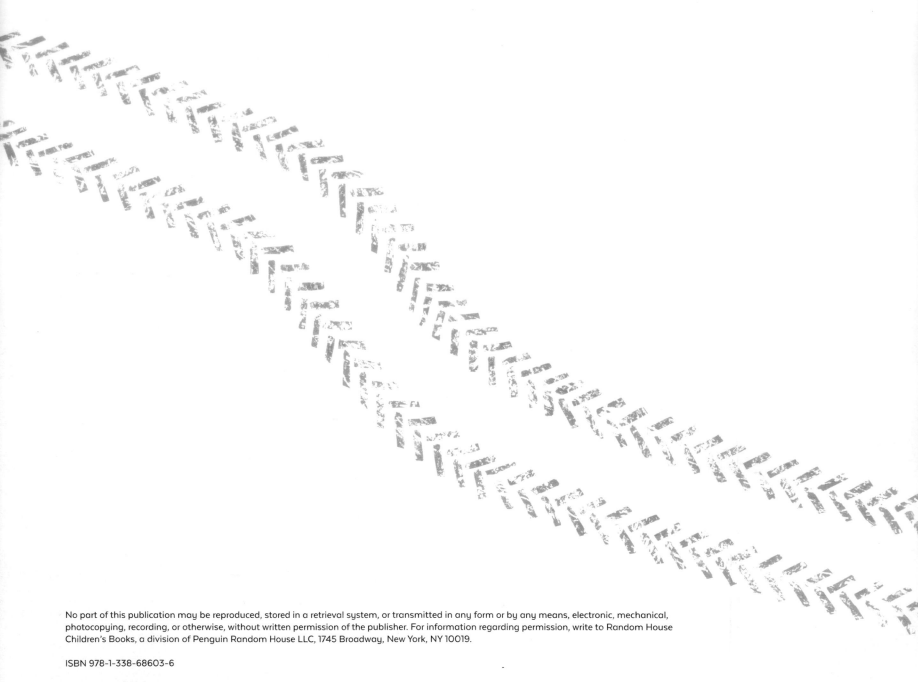

ISBN 978-1-338-68603-6

Copyright © 2018 by John F. A. Cena Entertainment, Inc. All rights reserved. Published by Scholastic Inc., 557 Broadway, New York, NY 10012, by arrangement with Random House Children's Books, a division of Penguin Random House LLC. SCHOLASTIC and associated logos are trademarks and/or registered trademarks of Scholastic Inc.

12 11 10 9 8 7 6 5 4 3 2   20 21 22 23 24 25

Printed in the U.S.A.   76

First Scholastic printing, September 2020